Red Riding Hood

Red Riding Hood

CHRISTOPHER COADY

London

Illustrations © 1991 Christopher Coady

First published in 1991 by **ABC**, All Books for Children,

a division of The All Children's Company Ltd

33 Museum Street, London WC1A 1LD

Printed and bound in Hong Kong

British Library Cataloguing in Publication Data

Coady, Christopher

Red Riding Hood.

I. Title

823.914 [J]

ISBN 1-85406-118-6

To my Mum and Dad
Thanks a lot

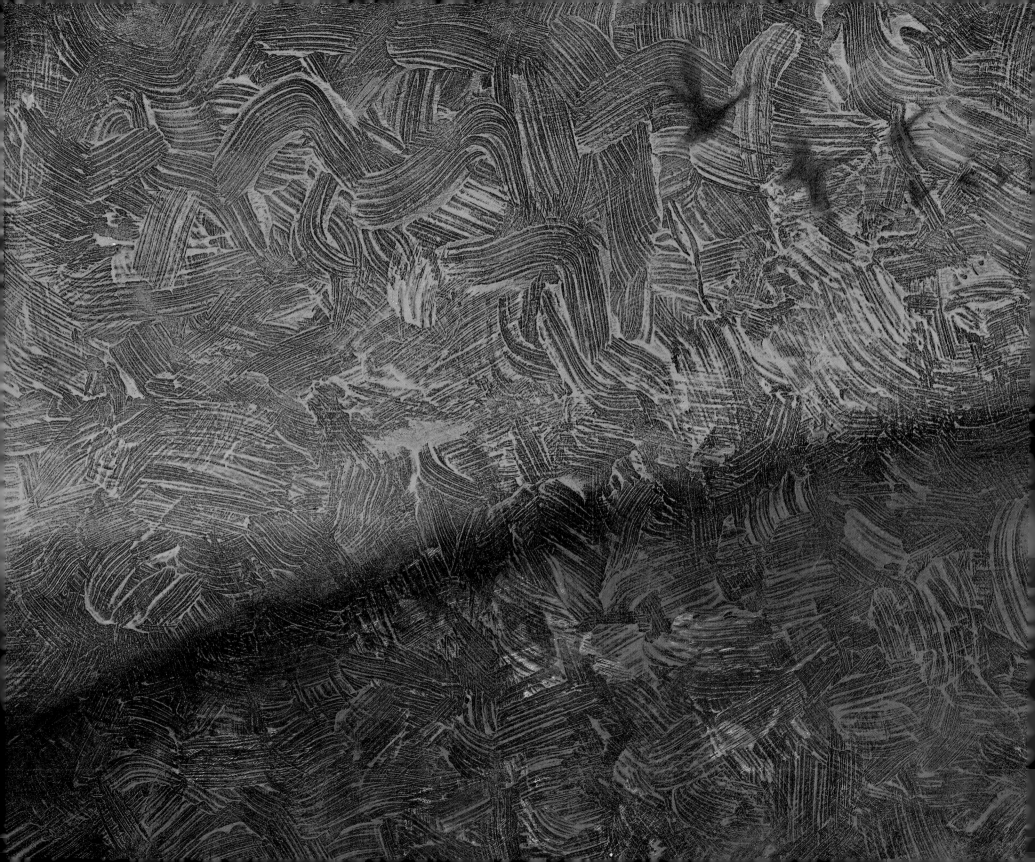

Once upon a time, in a distant village, lived a pretty but careless little girl. Her mother loved her dearly and made her a red cloak which suited her so well that everyone called her Red Riding Hood.

One day her mother baked some cakes and said to her daughter, "Go and take these to your grandmother, who has been ill. But beware of the wicked Wolf in the forest."

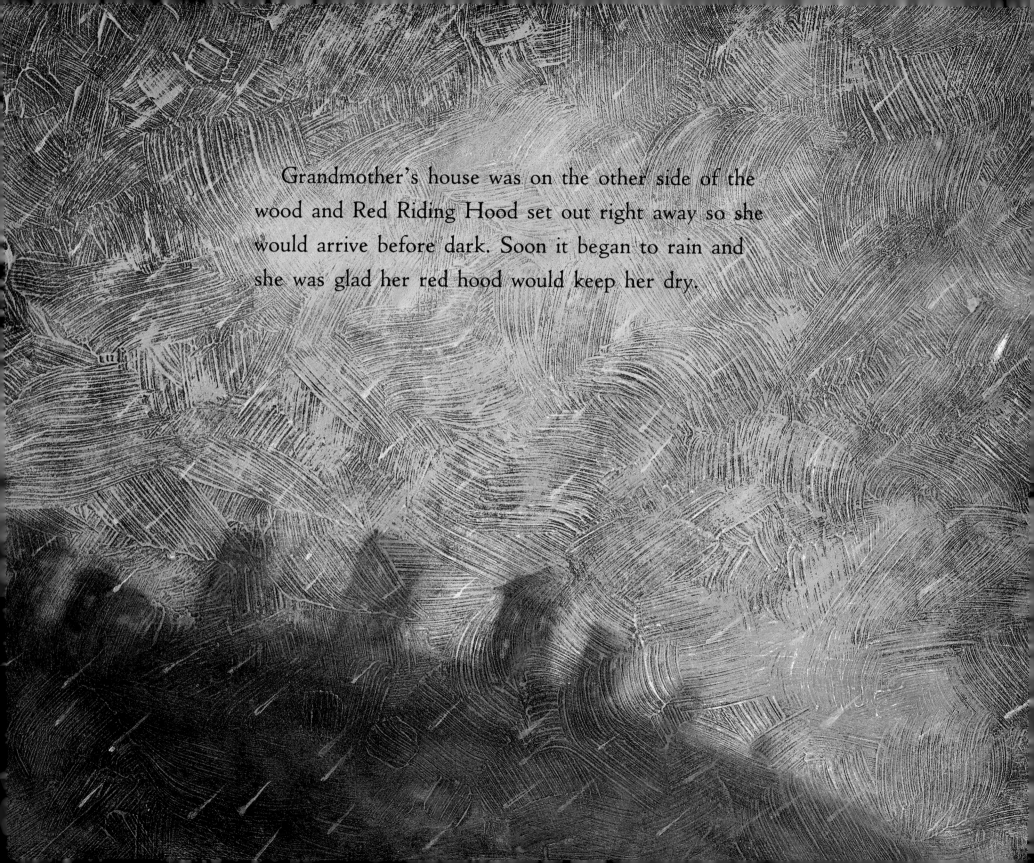

Grandmother's house was on the other side of the
wood and Red Riding Hood set out right away so she
would arrive before dark. Soon it began to rain and
she was glad her red hood would keep her dry.

As she walked into the darkening wood,
Red Riding Hood felt two eyes on her.

In a clearing, the Wolf came out, wary of
the woodcutters nearby. In a silky voice, he
asked Red Riding Hood where she was going.
"I'm taking some cakes to Grandma," she
replied, even though her mother had warned
her not to talk to the Wolf.

"She lives on the other side of the old mill,"
said Red Riding Hood.
"I shall visit her myself one day," said the
cunning Wolf, and disappeared into the shadows.

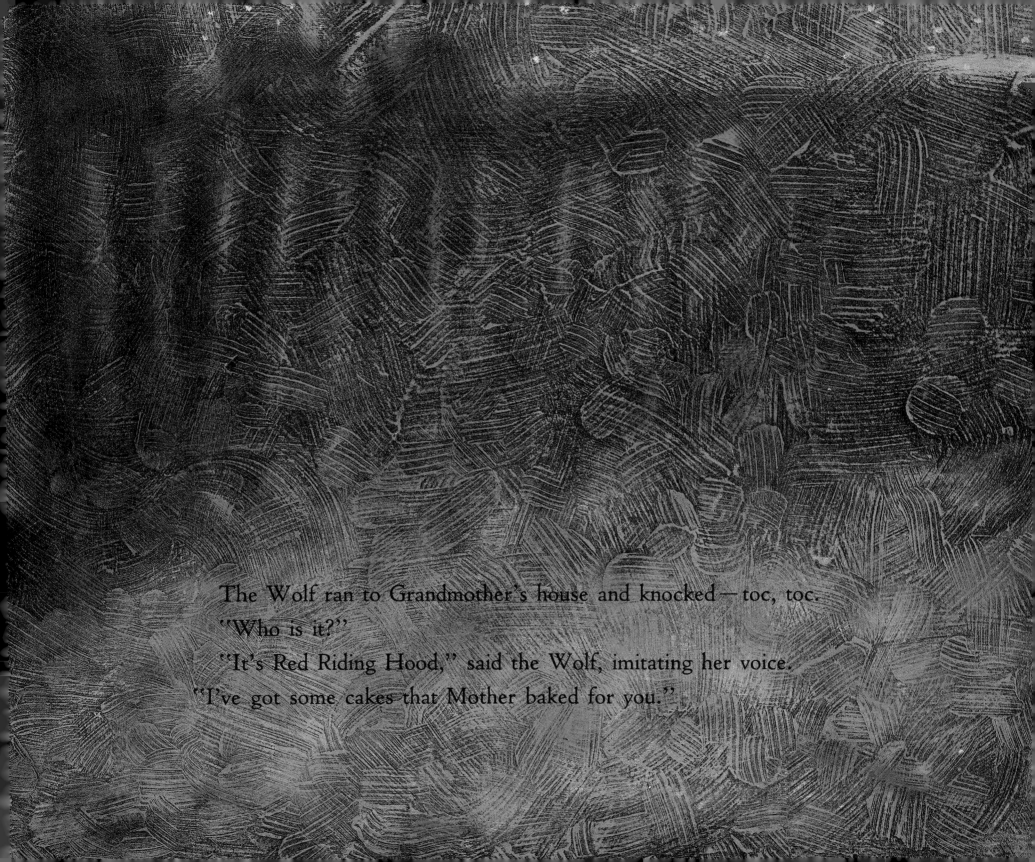

The Wolf ran to Grandmother's house and knocked—toc, toc.

"Who is it?"

"It's Red Riding Hood," said the Wolf, imitating her voice.

"I've got some cakes that Mother baked for you."

The grandmother called out, "Pull the
bobbin to lift up the latch."

The Wolf pulled the bobbin and the door
opened. He threw himself on to the poor
old woman and gobbled her up.

He then dressed himself in her nightdress,
put on her spectacles and got into bed.

Soon Red Riding Hood knocked at the door — toc, toc.

"Who is it?"

She was alarmed to hear the Wolf's deep tones but thought that Grandmother's voice sounded husky from her cold, and she replied, "Red Riding Hood and I've got some cakes that Mother baked for you."

In a gentler voice the Wolf called out,
"Pull the bobbin to lift up the latch."
Red Riding Hood pulled the bobbin
and the door opened.

"Put down the cakes," the Wolf called softly from
under the bedclothes, "and come lie down with me."
Red Riding Hood took off her cloak and got
into the bed. She was surprised to see what her
grandmother looked like in her nightdress.

"Grandmother, what big arms you've got!"
"All the better to hug you with, my child."

"Grandmother, what big ears you've got!"
"All the better to hear you with, my child."

"Grandmother, what big eyes you've got!"
"All the better to see you with, my child."

"Grandmother, what big teeth you've got!"

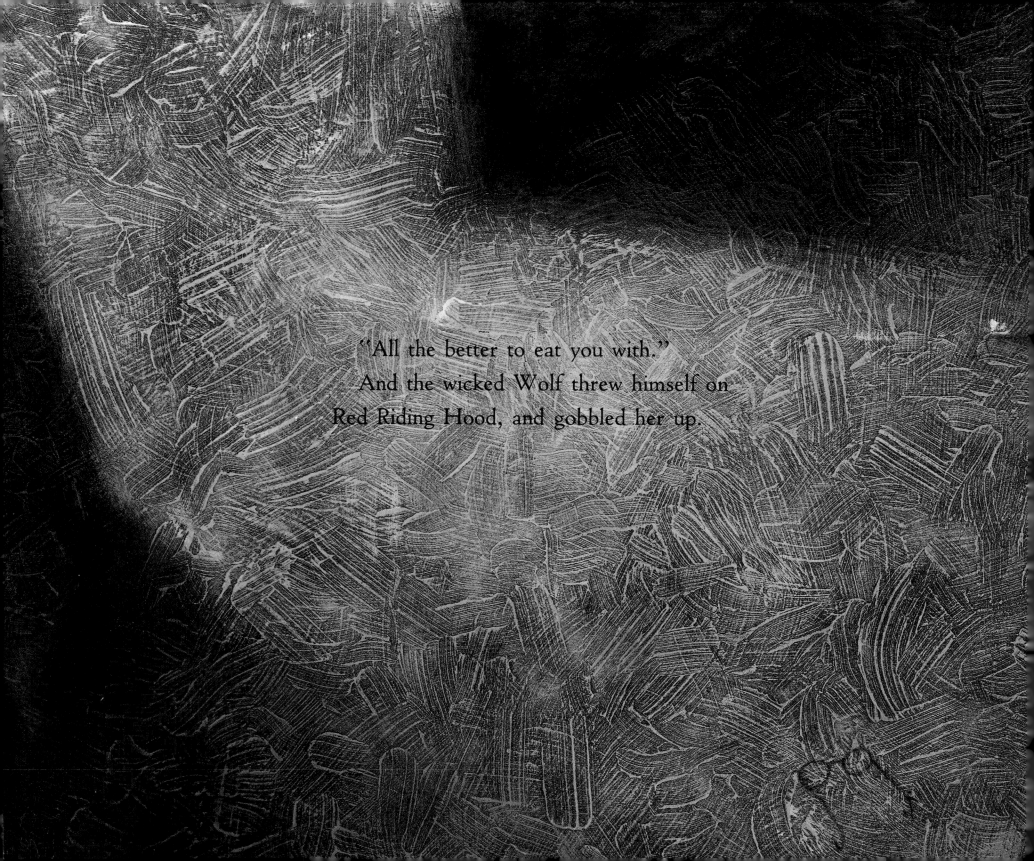

"All the better to eat you with."
And the wicked Wolf threw himself on
Red Riding Hood, and gobbled her up.

*F*rom that day until this, the sad story of Red Riding Hood has been a lesson to all little children. Sometimes wolves can be pleasant and charming, particularly when there are other people nearby. But those same wolves can follow careless little children down alleyways and even into houses where they can become very dangerous animals indeed.